THE MOOKSTER'S
MITZVAH MISHAPS

by Chana Nestlebaum
illustrated by George Berman

The Judaica Press, Inc.
New York

Library of Congress Catalog Card Number 91-75362

ISBN 0-910818-26-6 (hardcover)
ISBN 0-910818-27-4 (softcover)

This book—
along with the smiles it brings,
and the *mitzvos* it encourages—
is dedicated, in loving memory,
to my grandparents,
Bessie and Medill Goldstein
and Sadie Berman,
and to the memory
of my dear friend, Robin.

1

Back in the old days, there was just me—Ari—and my little sister Bahtya. Things were fine. We were both learning about *mitzvos* from Uncle Mendel's Sing-Along tapes and getting better at them every day.

Kibud av v'eim, being respectful to your father and mother, was one of our best *mitzvos*. For example, we always tried very hard to keep Mommy from getting lonely.

2

3

And we were very careful to make sure that Daddy always got plenty of exercise.

4

Another great *mitzvah* in our house was *hachnosas orchim*, welcoming guests. "Come on in and play!" we always said to all our friends.

5

And of course, we always remembered to say the
proper *brachos* before eating. In fact, we tried to
eat as much as we possibly could, just so we would
have more blessings to say.

Every night before going to sleep, we always remembered to recite the *Shema* as clearly, carefully, and S - L - O - W - L - Y as we could.

Then one day everything changed—the day we got *The Mookster*. At first, he was a regular baby with a regular name—Michah. All he did back then was eat, sleep, cry, and get his yucky diapers changed.

7

8

After a few days, my parents started calling him by funny nicknames. They said, "We want to see which one fits." They called him Mickey. Then Mookie. Then it became "The Mookster," and there it stayed.

Pretty soon, The Mookster became curious about the *mitzvos* Bahtya and I were doing. But he really couldn't do much—until he learned how to walk. Since then, life has been just one MISHAP after another.

9.

The Mookster must have been listening when
Mommy told me about *bal tashchis*, not wasting
things. I guess he thought the food in our garbage
pail was a big waste, so he decided to fix that.

10

11

At the end of *Shabbos*, when we made *Havdalah*, we never realized The Mookster was paying such close attention—until he tried it all by himself—on Tuesday afternoon!

One morning, Daddy took The Mookster to *shul* with him. That's where he learned the *mitzvah* of putting on *tefillin*, and he didn't waste any time figuring out how to do it all by himself.

12

13

Chesed, doing nice things for other people, is one of The Mookster's favorite *mitzvos*, but somehow, his chesed never really helps anyone. Like when he tries to wash the dishes . . .

Or cheer up Bahtya with a big, juicy kiss . . .

14

15

Or help me with my homework . . .

16

Or help Mommy clean the house.

We have lots of boxes in our house for *tzedakah*.
Bahtya explained to The Mookster that the money
in those boxes is for people who are poor and
hungry. So, he came up with his own way to help.

18

The Mookster is already getting very good at sharing. The only problem is what he shares, and with whom he shares it.

Whenever someone in our family catches cold, The Mookster is the first to do the *mitzvah* of *bikur cholim*, visiting sick people. Of course, he knows lots of unusual ways to cheer people up.

19

He's always looking for a chance to do *hashovas aveidah*, finding lost things and returning them to their owners. In fact, when things are lost in our house, The Mookster is always the first one we ask.

20

One time, The Mookster was about to step on a bug outside, but I stopped him and explained about *tzaar baalei chaim*, not causing pain to living things. Now he's best friends with the animals.

21

The Mookster loves doing *mitzvos* for the holidays. Every day, he prepares for *Pesach*. He's really good at *bedikas chometz*, when the kids hide pieces of bread and Daddy has to search everywhere for it.

22

And when *Pesach* is finally here, The Mookster searches and searches until he finds the *afikoman*.

23

Bahtya and I know that Daddy stays up all night on *Shavuos* learning *Torah*. But The Mookster tries to wake him up almost every night, just in case it is *Shavuos* and Daddy forgot.

24

Believe it or not, The Mookster is already starting to understand some of the *mitzvos* of *Yom Kippur*. Every Thursday night, when Mommy gives us spinach with our supper, he practices fasting.

Purim is another holiday that The Mookster loves to think about. Whenever Mommy leaves her makeup out on the dresser, The Mookster gets a chance to work on next year's costume.

26